CRYPTID BITS

JESS SIMMS

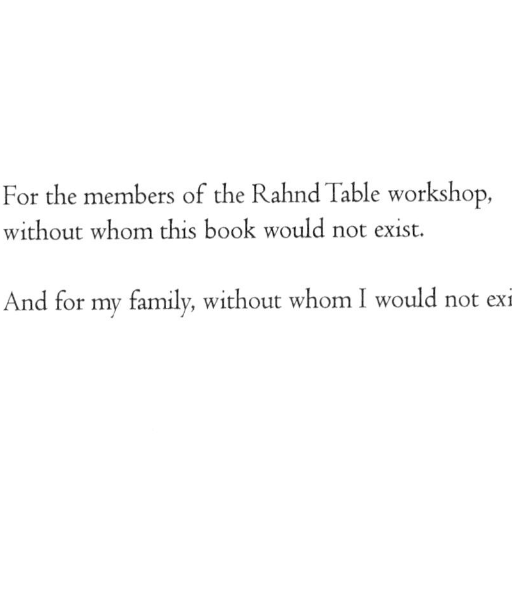

For the members of the Rahnd Table workshop,
without whom this book would not exist.

And for my family, without whom I would not exist.

TABLE OF CONTENTS

The Werewolf at the Farmer's Market

It must have been a full moon last Saturday because I ran into a werewolf at the night market. He was at one of the produce booths, a bag of arugula hanging from his right foreclaw and a head of romaine in his left palm. He was comparing the greens as though his paws were scales.

"Which one would you buy?" he asked as I perused the swiss chard, drawn in by the sunset colors of the stalks. He shook his shaggy head and growled, "I don't know what I'm doing. The doctor says my cholesterol's high, that I should eat more vegetables. He didn't mention how many damned kinds there are."

I told him I preferred arugula's peppery flavor but romaine was more versatile. The werewolf thanked me for my advice and tossed both options in his basket. I saw him once more on my way out. He was glaring at the display of a local orchard, where a dozen apple varieties vied for his attention.

"But what's the difference," he was asking, "between a Pink Lady and a Honeycrisp?"

The boy working the booth encouraged him to give one a try. The werewolf picked out the reddest fruit on the table and took an experimental bite.

7 Reasons Non-Cryptids Should Live in the Fairy District

When I tell other humans I live in the Fairy District, their reaction is like I just challenged a gorgon to a staring contest: somewhere between horror and awe. And I get it. If you only know it from the news, you probably think you'll be turned into a toad the second you cross Elm Street.

But that's not the whole story. The Fairy District is the fastest-growing neighborhood in the city, and its newly revitalized main street and port are favorite weekend destinations for all species. Here are just a few reasons why:

#1: It's an up-and-coming, livable neighborhood.
Tourists and visitors cause most of the trouble in the Fairy District, and usually it's because they do something stupid, like wandering around the dog park at night during a full moon. Yes, it's where most of the werewolves live but no, they don't hunt tourists—they buy their food from a grocery store, just like the rest of us (even if the stock at Rangda's Meats & Misc. is a bit different than what you'll see at the average human supermarket).

#2: It's got the best bars.

The Underbridge Tavern might be the only place in the city you can still get a shot and a beer for less than five bucks. Want a classier joint? The Riff Raff Club has been serving up craft cocktails since the prohibition era (just make sure you bring your ID—the bouncer's intense about carding). If you want an afterparty, follow the crowd leaving after last call. Even if you end up in a vampire's hilltop castle, things won't wind down until the sun comes up.

#3: You can get anything at the dockside markets.

The labyrinth of stalls along the riverwalk can be overwhelming on your first visit, but if you're looking for enchanted artifacts, exotic foods, or even just some bootleg DVDs, there's really nowhere better in the city.

#4: You'll eat the best pastries (if you can find them).

Treat Your Sylph was one of the neighborhood's best-kept secrets until its feature on the Food Network last year, but the air spirits who run the bakery haven't let their new-found fame go to their heads. They still use the same traditional recipes to make cakes, donuts, and other treats as light and airy as the cloud they're fried in. There's no set schedule for when or where their cloud will touch down any given day, so keep your eyes open for a fog bank trailing a line of hungry-looking locals any time you're out and about.

#5: It's fur-baby friendly.

Considering a good portion of the residents have fur, scales, or feathers (or a combination of all three), I suppose it's no surprise most establishments in the Fairy District welcome pets. They don't discriminate against non-cryptid pets, either. So long as your pup is well-behaved, you can take him everywhere from cafes to antique shops without a single stern talking to.

#6: The architecture is surreal (and affordable).

From skycastles to subterranean caverns, the variety of buildings available to rent in the Fairy District is remarkable. If you're looking to buy instead, you'll be pleasantly surprised by how much house (or cave, or tree) you get for your money.

#7: Every day is an adventure.

On any given day, you can have beer with a bigfoot, dine with a dragon, or take a swim with a selkie. The Bohemian culture of this vibrant neighborhood is its best quality, and the colorful locals will welcome you with open arms if you show up ready to have fun and make friends.

Comments on "7 Reasons Non-Cryptids Should Live in the Fairy District"

SidneyLou412

So fun! I love the Underbridge. Ug is such a sweetheart once you get to know him!

AgroArgonaut

treat your sylph kicks ass lol great list

LostLamb6525

Ummmm….do you NOT watch the news?!?? A solid 80-90% of the crime in this city is MONSTER related and you're telling regular people to move right INTO THE MIDDLE OF IT? This is DANGEROUS advice and I'm reporting you to have it taken down! Absolutely NO LAW-ABIDING, SELF-RESPECTING CITIZEN should EVER go to the Fairy District!!1! I went there once by accident and I have NEVER felt less safe in my LIFE!! The police really need to clean up the docks and send a message that this kind of culture will NOT be tolerated by the normal, hardworking people who call this city home.

ShenLongTheDragon

While I appreciate the intent of inclusion behind this piece, the human privilege of the author is problematic.

The "revitalization" of the Fae Business District mentioned in the introduction displaced dozens of residents who have lived there for generations, many of whom have fallen into homelessness as a result. I would encourage you to do more research into the history of the district before writing any more potentially damaging pieces such as this one.

Matt869581038

I simply wanted to write down a quick word to say thanks to you for those wonderful tips and hints you are showing on this site. I've got a tip for you and your readers, as well! Something that has completely turned my life around and made me happier and more fulfilled in my bedroom and my confidence.

It's called CentaurX and it really works, guys, I'm serious. You're going to get a bigger size and more stamina in just hours after you start taking this natural supplement. Basically think about the phrase "hung like a…" and you know what centaurs are half of, right?

Here's the real secret though, guys, is that right now you can try it out for two months basically free if you just type in the code CRX60 when you checkout at CentaurX.com. Not sure how long it's going to last at those prices so hit it up now!

STRIKING BROWNIES TAKE TO THE STREETS

The more than 400 brownies employed by local hotel chain Xenios Hospitality LLC have officially announced a strike. Crowds of striking employees—as well as supporters who have turned out in solidarity—formed outside all five Xenios Hospitality-owned locations early this morning.

Discussions between the Brownie Union and Xenios Hospitality have at times turned heated since the contract between them expired in January. Talks stalled last Tuesday, when Xenios CEO Janus Masters reportedly stormed away from the negotiating table, according to claims by Brownie Union representative Mim Ninnins. Ninnins announced the strike later that day, calling it "an inevitable consequence of this company's policy of looking down on us but never looking at us."

Masters has not been reached for comment since the strike commenced. Demands from the striking employees were read aloud today outside each affected hotel and have also been published on the local Brownie Union website.

The Brownie Union Has Published Their Strike Demands and They're Absolutely Eye-Opening

Traditional brownie culture makes them easy to exploit. For one thing, they'll literally work for peanuts (as long as they're baked into a pastry). That, combined with their supernaturally speedy cleaning skills, is why they now make up more than half the housekeeping staff, not just at Xenios Hospitality but across the city. It's understandable if you didn't know that. Brownies, as a rule, go out of their way to not be seen, which makes this strike even more intriguing. Neither side has shared many details of what prompted the strike, but the Brownie Union's demands certainly paint a picture:

The brownies employed by Xenios Hospitality LLC hereby make the following demands:

1) Fair pastries for fair work.

2) Food left over after continental breakfasts and other buffet services will be redistributed to the brownie population if it will otherwise be discarded.

3) Employee bathrooms must be made accessible to all employees. No employee should be expected to bring personal stools or stepladders in order to reach the sink.

4) Brownie employees will not be singled out and terminated for playing tricks on multi-day guests.

5) Brownie employees who turn bogart as a result of mistreatment by guests, coworkers, or supervisors will not be subject to termination.

6) Bogart rehabilitation therapy must be included under the employee health plan, and eligible for worker's compensation should the turn occur as a result of mistreatment by guests or management.

7) Brownie employees will not be subject to termination for absences related to attending bogart rehabilitation therapy, regardless of the impetus or location of their turn.

Sounds pretty reasonable to me. What do you all think? Let me know if you agree in the comments!

Comments on "The Brownie Union Has Published Their Strike Demands and They're Absolutely Eye-Opening"

LostLamb6525

You've got to be shitting me. No human employee could ever get away with playing a trick on a customer. And WTF is "bogart rehabilitation therapy"? Snowflakes looking for a handout, let them walk and find work elsewhere. Good on the hotel management for not giving in to these ridiculous demands.

FieryFreja5

Sounds like it's about damn time brownies stood up for their rights! I know a lot of them live paycake-to-paycake, any orgs out there helping make sure their families stay fed while they're fighting for their rights?

> **BaetheFae88**
>
> lol we should organize a bake off. All benefits (and baked goods) go to the brownies!
>
> > **FieryFreja5**
> >
> > Love it! What should we call it?
> >
> > > **SwampSkunk420**
> > >
> > > Get Baked for Brownies

ShenLongTheDragon

Ha! Think that might send the wrong impression.

BaetheFae88

Or the right impression…?

ShenLongTheDragon

This is a fantastic idea, truly. I'm going to see what we can do to start organizing things, DM me if you want to be involved.

LostLamb6525

Oh please. You know they're just going to go back to stealing food like they always have. "Honest brownie" is an oxymoron.

Yowl! Reviews for Gorgon Sisters Hair Salon

SugarplumPixie

I came to this salon last Friday because my usual spot down the street was booked. Big mistake!!! I will NEVER step foot in this establishment again!!

The problems started the second I walked in. First I noticed the smell. More like a pet store than a hair salon (?!?). There were three stylists working and not one of them even looked at me when I came through the door! When I finally got an employee's attention her hair ACTUALLY HISSED at me—and she didn't even apologize! THEN I realized there wasn't a single mirror anywhere. I was like WTF, how do you have a hair salon without any mirrors? When I asked how I was supposed to see my hair, the stylist snapped I should just take a selfie with my phone "like everybody else". Serious nerve for her to treat me like an idiot after she'd COMPLETELY failed at customer service the ENTIRE interaction.

Cut and color were fine but I would never recommend Gorgon Sisters to anyone unless I absolutely hated them! If you're looking for a good stylist Cutlantis is just a block away on Water Street, go there instead!

BaetheFae88

I was dubious after reading other reviews, but I have to say I was pleasantly surprised by my appointment yesterday. My stylist gave me exactly what I asked for and her hair was well-behaved throughout our interaction. And the décor is stunning! Love the columns and all the white marble—their policy on reflective surfaces is a bit bizarre, but that's not enough to keep me from coming back.

Ammit_Devourer_of_the_Dead

Nowhere else in the city does scale and fur care with the finesse and expertise you'll get at Gorgon Sisters. First came in for a scale buff during a rough shedding and they threw in a mane shampooing no extra charge. I've been going back ever since, can't recommend enough.

PerseusOfSeriphus19

Too many snakes.

LOCAL ACTIVIST, DRAGON ANNOUNCES CANDIDACY

Shen Long officially threw his name into the ring for the 13th District State House primaries Thursday night. The announcement confirmed social media speculation regarding Long's political aspirations, which had reached a peak after online news outlet Cryptid Watch posted footage of a supposed campaign planning meeting between Long and fellow organizers.

Long, who is a 30-foot dragon, the Bringer of the Rain, and a long-time advocate for workers' rights, was a scheduled speaker at the Fight for Fifteen rally in downtown's Stoker Square. He spoke of his ongoing work to raise the minimum wage and drew attention to the brownie strike at the nearby Olympus Grande before confirming his candidacy.

The crowd response to Long's announcement was overwhelmingly positive, surging when Long addressed criticisms of his wealth, which he called "equally speciest and specious," adding, "These CEOs like to point at my hoard like it justifies their greed, but the truth is I pay every member of my staff a wage well above the fifteen dollar minimum we're asking for. I'd tell them to interrogate their own treasure piles before they start pulling out the pitchforks and torches."

Long declined to comment on what role cryptid equality would play in his campaign, but assured reporters his full platform would be available on his website early next week.

The Interview with a Vampire (on Channel 6 Morning News)

Channel 6: It's time now for our Local Voices segment, where we feature the unique citizens who make up our city. Today we're talking to Louise, who is—as I understand it—the only undead female mortician in our town. Is that right, Louise?

Louise: That's correct, yes.

Channel 6: What was it that drew you to such an unusual career?

Louise: I like to say the job chose me. I started as a night cleaner and just fell in love with the atmosphere—you'd be surprised how hard it is to find a windowless workspace.

Channel 6: And plenty of coffins around if you feel like taking a nap.

Louise: [polite chuckle.]

Channel 6: Now what exactly is it that you do?

Louise: My main job is preparing bodies for funerals and wakes. It's a service for the living, really, making the deceased look like the person they love and remember.

Channel 6: What would you say is the best part of working as a mortician?

Louise: Knowing I've helped the survivors grieve. It's also a very peaceful job. You get a lot of time alone to think, which some people might see as a bad thing but I appreciate my solitude. Small talk loses its appeal after a few centuries.

Channel 6: And I suppose it's an easy way to get free snacks.

Louise: I'm sorry?

Channel 6: Well you have to drain the blood anyway, right?

Louise: Oh. Vampires drink live blood, so no, I've never—and would never.

Channel 6: I was just joking, you can relax. Now, as an undead individual—

Louise: Vampire.

Channel 6: Excuse me?

Louise: You can say what I am.

Channel 6: Well it looks like that's all the time we have for today. Join us in the kitchen after the break, where a local celebrity chef is going to teach us how he makes his iconic blood pudding. Sounds delicious, right? We'll be right back after these messages.

Banshee and the Siouxsies Play the Underbridge Tavern

The head bartender at the Underbridge is a real troll. Not like those pretenders who hang out at the Riff Raff Club, with their neon hair and the gems in their belly buttons. We're talking a wart-nosed, hunched-backed, turns-to-stone-in-sunlight, verified troll—perfect for the Underbridge, is basically what I'm saying. His name's Ug, if you're ever there and need to get his attention. Ug's got a lot of skills, but observation isn't one of them.

Anyway, you should've seen Ug the other night working the Banshee and the Siouxsies concert. You'd think a crypt metal crowd would be low-maintenance—beers and shots, a few blood-based cocktails—but Banshee's new mainstream fanbase has bougie tastes and Ug's not exactly a mixologist. This one siren I swear was standing at the bar for two whole songs, screeching out the names of obscure drinks and shots and liqueurs while Ug blinked, looking more confused with every word until the siren finally huffed and said,

"Just make me something good. And strong, but not, like, *strong* strong, like I don't want it to *taste* like it's strong, you know? And a little fruity but not too sweet. Do you have mint? Or rose water. Something that tastes like spring."

Whatever Ug served her, it sent her back to her table, much to the relief of everyone at the bar.

The show? It was alright. Banshee only broke five glasses. Kind of felt like she was phoning it in, like now that they're popular a joint like the Underbridge isn't worth their time. Or maybe they were just having an off night. Either way, I doubt they'll be playing the Underbridge again any time soon. And I'm sure Ug's plenty fine with that.

SHEN LONG WINS 13th DISTRICT PRIMARIES IN NARROW VICTORY

Shen Long was declared the winner of the 13th District Democratic State House Representative nomination early Thursday morning after a two-day delay in results. It is the first time in national history a cryptid has received a major party nomination for state office.

Initially seen as a dark horse candidate, Long's campaign picked up momentum through April but seemed to stall when the candidate, who is a 30-foot Western dragon, became a person of interest in the investigation of three missing children, one of whose charred bodies was discovered in the vicinity of the rear entrance to Long's summer treasure hoard.

When questioned about the case, Long said, "My heart goes out to all those affected by this tragedy, but the fact is the police questioned me with minimal cause, wasting resources on interrogating cryptids that could have gone to finding the two children still missing. This investigation is only further proof that I need to continue my work fighting for equality for all citizens."

Local Police Chief Lom Franks announced before the election that Long was questioned in an informational capacity only, though several local news outlets erroneously reported the House candidate as a suspect. It was uncertain how the investigation would affect his polling numbers.

Long now turns his sights to taking on incumbent Republican representative George Saint in November. Defeating Saint is likely to prove a challenge for Long given the 13th District's historically red leanings.

"My team's thinking about it already, I'm sure," Long told reporters. "For my part I think I'll take a few days to enjoy this moment. This is a big step in the evolution of attitudes toward cryptids and I'm proud of my city making history today."

The Mummy Returns (to Pick Up His Drycleaning)

Mummies are legit the worst customers. They always have these huge lists of special instructions—written in hieroglyphs they know damn well you can't read—then glare at you with their shriveled arms folded like they're just waiting for you to make a mistake.

And gods save you if you do mess up. Last week, the werewolf working the register gave a mummy someone else's laundry—she read the tag upside down is all I can figure; she's always a bit airheaded when there's a waning gibbous—and I had the bad luck to be at the counter when he came back, dead-set on retribution. He threw the bag on the counter yelling for his bandages and a refund.

"It's preposterous!" the mummy shouted. "My wraps are made of 500-count Egyptian cotton. How could anyone confuse them for these rags?" Then he demanded to see the manager and launched into a tirade with lots of back in my days about work ethic and pyramids.

He calmed down once he had his laundry, a refund, and a credit for twenty bucks on his next visit. The most awkward part was that the wraith whose clothes he'd gotten by mistake materialized during his rant. They lurked in the shadows beside the counter, radiating malice, until the mummy lurched stiffly toward the door.

"Rags?" the wraith muttered as I handed over their laundry, "I've got sheets with a higher thread count than his bandages."

The mummy stopped and looked back but thankfully didn't make a stink. Which was surprising, honestly. He seemed like he was in a cursing mood.

Pros and Cons of Going to the Movies with a Bigfoot

Pro: If you go with him, you can suggest sitting in the back row. And if you can't get him to the back row—he just can't see from there, you see, he really should get a new prescription but who has time for the eye doctor, what with all the activities the kids are in, the extra hours at the office—at least you're sitting next to him, so you can still see the screen.

Con: That smell his fur has is even worse inside and up close for that long. And if it's been raining? Like a wet dog covered in river mud standing in a musty basement.

Pro: He's usually so happy someone's asked him to hang out he'll let you pick the movie without putting up a fight. Remember that time you took him to see King Kong? Wasn't until halfway through you realized it might've been uncomfortable for him. You still feel a bit guilty about that.

Con: It takes him forever at concessions. Every time, he squints up at the menu, scratching his cheek fur—like he's never heard of a movie snack, even though you went through this same ritual with him last month, and the one before that—then asks whatever poor kid's behind the counter if they know whether the nacho cheese sauce is gluten-free—and does it use real dairy?—and if he can read the ingredients on the candy boxes before—finally—settling on a large combo and a box of Raisinets, like he always does.

Pro: He always regrets the large popcorn he bought before the movie even starts and insists you help him eat it, so you won't need to shell out much for snacks.

Con: He always wants to get dinner afterwards and you have to make some excuse why you can't, which you're pretty sure he always knows is an excuse, because you're not the kind of person who has much going on Saturday nights. You've tried avoiding the problem by suggesting later showings but he'll only go to matinees. Theaters are too crowded at night, he says, which—to be fair—maybe suggests he's more self-conscious of his height and odor than you've given him credit for.

Pro: You wife hangs out with his wife, so when she mentions how you voluntarily went to the movies with him—and how happy he was to have friends for once—it'll earn you brownie points. Plus he does have those season tickets for the Scarlet Dragons. Maybe you'll take him up on his next dinner offer. Hell, you might even let him pick the movie.

Every Banshee and the Siouxsies Album Ranked

After *Kill the Messenger* won Best New Album at the Grammys, I'm hearing lots of people calling Banshee and the Siouxsies their favorite new band—which is funny, considering they've been a fixture of the crypt metal scene since CryptFest 2003. To get these newcomers up to speed (and spur a lively debate among the band's die-hard fanbase), here's a ranking of their discography from worst to best:

Keening for the Dead (2003): 3/10

Hardcore Banshee fans are pulling out the pitchforks, but let's be honest: the Banshee and the Siouxsies debut is damn-near unlistenable. Basically you're in for 45 minutes of high-pitched screeching over a thrash metal beat.

Concerto for Harp and Nitroglycerin (2011): 6/10

Why do metal bands always think they need a concept album? *Concerto* is set in a dystopian post-apocalyptic future where cryptids have been rounded into camps. It's a cool idea but heavy-handed in the execution, with its cliched insertions of folk songs and overt political messaging (which, sure, there's some political undertones to other Banshee songs, but at least you can dance to them).

Shattered (2015): 7/10

There are some great tracks on this album. "Bean She" is an anthem of female empowerment and "Fairy Stories" is one of the best break-up songs of our generation. The songs between the hits sound like filler, though, and there's no cohesion from one track to the next.

Kill the Messenger (2019): 8/10

It's easy to see why this album is the band's first award-winner. Every track is strong individually and they flow together beautifully—almost too beautifully, in fact, and that's my only complaint: it's over-produced and missing Banshee's usual grit.

Bog Standard (2007): 10/10

This ironically titled album is anything but ordinary. *Bog Standard* is one of those rare albums with no weak tracks, from the plaintive opening wails of "Solstice" to the 7/8-time shenanigans of "Stoats and Weasels."

Comments on "Every Banshee and the Siouxsies Album Ranked"

BaetheFae88

OMG Ann Wilde is sooooo hot!!! Luv Banshee and the Siouxsies.

PixieDustBunny

You think Concerto is their most political album?!?!? Kill the Messenger is obviously about worker's rights if you have the brains to look through the allegory. Clearly you're not as big a fan as you claim to be.

DocJekyllMD

Banshee and the Siouxsies sold out after Bog Standard. Real crypt metal fans listen to Great Wight.

BAKEAID FESTIVAL TO SUPPORT STRIKING BROWNIES

What started as a joke on social media will become a reality this Saturday, thanks mostly to the work of local politician and 30-foot dragon Shen Long. The event dubbed BAKEAid will take place in Hyde Park, across the street from the Olympus Grande, one of five local hotels whose brownie employees have been on strike for several weeks.

The most prominent name that will perform at the festival is Grammy-winning local band Banshee and the Siouxsies. Frontwoman Ann Wilde—the titular Banshee of the popular all-cryptid metal band—is a vocal advocate for worker's rights and has partnered with Long before on community projects.

Along with musical performances, BAKEAid will have booths for more than 25 local eateries. All entry proceeds will support the striking employees, many of whom have struggled to feed their families as this prolonged strike continues.

Event organizers are hoping to raise awareness of the ongoing strike and put extra pressure on hotel management to agree to the union's demands. The properties are owned by Xenios Hospitality LLC, who had previously come under fire after several guests accused hotel staff of enchanting them after they threatened to leave negative reviews.

In his initial statement when the strike began, Xenios CEO Janus Masters indicated he would convert to a non-brownie cleaning staff rather than sign the new contract. He has not commented publicly on the BAKEAid festival.

The Wraith at the Riff Raff Club

I don't believe in ghosts. That's what I told the wraith checking IDs for the Actual Dragons show at the Riff Raff Club last Friday night.

"Your belief is immaterial," the wraith replied—they talk like that; they've been guarding this same door since about 1885—"Lacking proof that you have achieved the national age for imbibing spirits, I cannot permit you entry into this establishment."

I never seem to get on well with spectral beings. On the way to the club, a seemingly benign conversation with the revenant driving my Uber turned heated after he took offense when I used solid to mean good. It got so awkward I forgot my bag in his backseat.

The wraith was not sympathetic when I explained my predicament. "Your irresponsibility is not just cause for an exemption from the law," they said.

I could see there would be no reasoning with them. I considered slipping through them but we've all seen the story about the frat kid who tried that last summer. Who knows if he'll ever get out of that psych ward. I decided to cut my losses and head home. I saw Actual Dragons when they opened for Great Wight a couple years ago. They put on a good show and all, but they're not worth that kind of trouble.

The Chef From the Black Lagoon (On Channel 6 Morning News)

Channel 6: You're all set to show off your culinary skills at your next dinner party—then the dietary requests come in, and you have to find a meal to satisfy both vegans and vampires. What can you do? We've called upon our favorite foodie to help answer that question. Eric Grendel is the executive chef of the Black Lagoon, the Fairy District's only Michelin-starred restaurant. Eric, welcome back to Channel 6.

Eric: It's good to be back.

Channel 6: So last time we talked I offered you a challenge.

Eric: The impossible dinner party.

Channel 6: [laughs] I don't think that's how I phrased it, but that's what it comes down to! How do you make a meal that everyone can eat—and enjoy!—without cooking a different dish for everyone?

Eric: Well, Wendy, this is something I deal with on a daily basis. My main goal in opening Black Lagoon was to serve high-end cuisine for any dietary needs. It's personal for me—my oldest daughter, she's deathly allergic to both algae and alligator, which makes it pretty challenging to cook traditional swamp dishes at home.

Channel 6: Oh, I'll bet. And if you're hosting dinner— you've got a werewolf coming, a minotaur, a few humans but one of them's gluten free and another's doing Keto—

Eric: First of all, don't try to cook one meal that will appeal to every palate and culture. Because that is actually impossible.

Channel 6: So what's the solution?

Eric: Small plates. Call it tapas, call it dim sum— doesn't matter. There are other advantages to this style of meal, too. You can farm out some of the work, for one.

Channel 6: Almost like a potluck?

Eric: Except you don't have to ask every guest to bring something. Plan with a couple of friends to each prepare a dish or two. And play to their strengths—if your minotaur buddy offers to cook, let them make the meat course, don't ask them to prepare the salad.

Channel 6: Now I know our viewers expect you to do a little cooking when you stop by. We're going to commercial while we move to the kitchen, but what are you going to make when we come back?

Eric: I've got two dishes. For the meat-eaters out there, we're going to make sweetbread and haggis—a crowd-pleaser for canids and avians. Then we're going to go straight veggie—straight vegan, in fact—with a vegetable Biryani with a mandrake-lavender chutney. And I've got a bonus, one I think you'll particularly like, Wendy: my special Bloody Mary recipe, done two ways, with one method that's perfect if you've got blood-drinkers on your invite list.

Channel 6: If that's not enough to make people stay tuned, I don't know what is!

HOUSE CANDIDATE SUES OPPOSITION OVER ANTI-CRYPTID AD CAMPAIGN

House Candidate Shen Long has sued opponent George Saint in response to the latest installment in a series of attack ads. Running under the collective title "Slay the Serpent," the first of the five ads in the series debuted in mid-June.

In their official statement, Long's campaign stated they followed the ad sequence from its launch but are taking action now because "this latest iteration crossed the line from political mud-slinging into a harmful depiction of dragons as a species."

The ad in question depicts George Saint in knight's armor stabbing a fire-breathing dragon. The main point of contention is a segment in which the dragon incinerates a bound woman wearing a placard that reads "Family Values."

Long—who is himself a 30-foot dragon—said of the ads, "I accept that by running for public office I open myself up to attacks. In this ad, however, Saint portrays dragons as violent and dangerous, and that attitude has no place in our modern political dialogue."

Long also criticized the fourth ad in the series, which showed a dragon with an exaggerated Fu Man-Chu mustache in an opium den. As Long explained, "My ancestry is Bavarian, not Asian. The original family surname, Lange, was changed to Long by a typographic error when my grandparents emigrated to the United States. Anyone can see from my wings and spiked tail that I'm of European descent. Using Eastern stereotypes to discredit me not only demonstrates an atrocious lack of sensitivity, it shows my opponent didn't do his due diligence to get his facts straight."

Long also criticized the media's coverage of his candidacy, saying, "One report described me as the Bringer of the Rains. That title belongs to Japanese serpentine dragon Shin Ryu, the meteorologist for Channel 6 who—as far as I know—has no political aspirations."

Long's legal team has not yet revealed what damages are being sought in the civil suit.

Overheard Conversation between a Bigfoot and a Swampman in the Express Check-Out Line

I was reading the covers of the tabloids in the checkout aisle—Batboy's in the news again; that kid knows how to make headlines—when I saw the bigfoot who was next in line inching closer to the swampman ahead of him, sniffing conspicuously.

"Do you mind?" the swampman finally asked, seaweed dreadlocks flopping as he turned.

"It's just—that bog stench," the bigfoot answered. "You don't have it. Is that Fresh'n'Clean shampoo on the belt the one you use?"

"This is dog shampoo," said the swampman, picking up the bottle. "It's for Tiny, my Chupacabra. Little bastard got himself sprayed by a skunk last night."

The bigfoot hesitated before asking, "But Tiny— how does he smell after you bathe him?"

"Good enough. I'll tell you what I do, though," the swampman said, voice dropping conspiratorially as he leaned in—then jerked back again; the bigfoot's need for odor control advice was indeed dire—"Once a week, I get my seaweed damp and dust it all over in baking soda. Let it sit a few minutes and rinse yourself off with a mix of vinegar and lemon juice. Keeps me smelling fresh for days."

"I'm just not sure that would work on fur," the bigfoot mused, hefting the shampoo again to ask, "You found this in the pet care aisle?"

The swampman said he did. The bigfoot thanked him profusely, nearly bowling me over on his way to the aisles.

BLOOD+DRIVE

The Vampire at the Blood Drive

I went to the blood drive yesterday and saw them turn away a vampire. He really wanted to donate, I guess. He made kind of a scene about it.

"I'm a tax-paying American," he kept saying. "My blood's just as good as anyone else's."

The nurse implored him to stay calm. He wasn't being rejected for his undead orientation, she told him; it was his travel history, the recent trip to Romania he'd indicated on his registration form.

"You could be carrying a blood-borne pathogen even our detailed screenings can't pick up," the nurse said. "It's important to keep our blood supply safe, for both our living and undead patients."

I was filling out my own forms while I eavesdropped, checking NO on the question about travel with a stab of regret and jealousy; it had been years since I'd left the country.

The nurse's answer mollified the vampire. She gave him a list of upcoming blood drives in the area and encouraged him to return once enough time had elapsed since his trip. The vampire said he would most certainly be back. His phrasing sounded a tad menacing, but I don't think he meant anything by it.

HOUSE CANDIDATE SHEN LONG APOLOGIZES FOR RACIST COMMENTS

Shen Long apologized to the Asian dragon community today in a press conference televised live on Channel 6 News at Noon.

"I sincerely apologize for my lack of sensitivity when crafting my response to Mr. Saint's advertisements," Long said. "I only meant to point out to my opponent—and others who are not aware—that dragons are a diverse species whose origins are not limited to any one continent. But I can certainly see, in hindsight, how my comments could imply I was offended to be compared to Chinese dragons. For that, I am deeply sorry."

In response to questions, Long went on to say, "It was never my intention to insult the great tradition of Asian dragons both within our community and around the world, which is arguably longer and richer than that of Bavarian, German, Celtic, and other European dragon cultures."

For most of his campaign, Shen Long has been the darling of both local progressives and the cryptid community, being as he is a 30-foot dragon, the first of his species to receive a major party nomination in the United States.

The comments in question were made in response to an ad campaign by Long's opponent, George Saint. A lawsuit brought by Long's campaign was recently settled out of court. The offending ads were pulled from television as a provision of the settlement.

Overheard Conversation Between a Minotaur and a Werewolf on the Bus to Downtown

Each of them had a seat to themselves, the minotaur in front, turned to converse with the werewolf in the row behind. His weight bent the seat back to a deep angle.

"I remember when my father took me on my first hunt," the werewolf said. "I'd looked forward to it for months, and that day—how my heart raced for the chase! How much sweeter the meat! But Junior? He acts like it's some old-fashioned tradition. It's like he sees it as a chore."

"At least your kids eat meat," the minotaur replied, dolefully. "My daughter's a vegetarian."

"As in she only eats vegetables?" the werewolf asked, and when the minotaur nodded, said, "But why?"

The minotaur shifted his weight. The seat groaned ominously. He said, "I can't figure it out. At first I thought it was a phase but it's been almost a year now. It's that bigfoot girl she's friends with who put the idea in her head. She's a bad influence."

The werewolf shook his head. "I ate some vegetables recently. I don't know what anyone sees in them."

"It's unnatural," said the minotaur.

"Like a werewolf who won't hunt," the werewolf agreed. "You know Junior turns twelve next month and I don't think he's ever seen a carcass? I'm starting to think we never should've moved out of the forest. I mean, Linda and I both have great jobs, and the schools are much better, but is all that really worth it if we lose our nature?"

The minotaur rumbled commiseration.

Yowl! Reviews for Aladdin's Lamp Bar and Bistro

L4dyL4z4ru$

Stopped in for a few drinks at the bar after work the other night. Place has a nice ambiance, enough stuff on the walls to look at without it feeling cluttered and a good light/noise level—I'd give it a 5/5 for the feel. Great happy hour specials—all mixed drinks are $5 and they're not bottom-shelf, either. They don't quite have the 1001 drinks they advertise but their cocktail list is pretty robust. I started with a classic whiskey sour just to feel them out then got two of their specialty drinks, The Drop of Honey and the Blood and Sand, which had a pleasant tang and might have been my favorite. I'll give the drinks a 4/5 overall, and a 4.5 for value.

Staff was friendly overall. Bartender wasn't especially talkative but he was efficient and had a heavy pour, so I can't complain. The only weird thing was I think the bartender cut me off after three drinks. I say "I think" because he never said anything to me but when I tried to order a fourth he wouldn't even look at me. He was still serving other customers, and to be fair the bar was packed so maybe he was just in the weeds, but it really seemed like he was ignoring me on purpose.

Didn't order any of the food so I can't speak to that but for cocktails, I'd both recommend and come back.

LostLamb6525

Came here for dinner with my girlfriends the other night and had a TERRIBLE experience. All three of my friends, the waiter took their order and their drinks showed up, like, a second later, but he COMPLETELY ignored me! Just poof, disappeared and never came back to the table. And I don't think it was a coincidence I was the only one wearing a George Saint hat. I am sick of all these businesses letting their employees politics interfere with serving customers! We left without paying and will NOT be coming back.

FieryFreja5

I've yet to taste a dish here I don't like! The chefs use all locally-grown, organic produce and you can really taste it. The only reason Aladdin's Lamp has such a low rating is from people bashing the service just because they don't understand jinn culture. I'm sick of these tourists coming to the Fairy District and then getting offended when they have to adapt to local traditions. Ignore any review that calls the servers g---- (jinn, jinni, or djinn are the correct terms) or that complains about being "ignored" by staff. A seven-year-old could figure out you have to rub a lamp to get a jinn's attention. Do these idiots even look at the name of the restaurant?

I know I went off on a bit of a rant there but this is one of the best spots in the city and it annoys me when people badmouth it. Definitely recommend it to anyone who wants an authentic experience.

VOTE
SHEN LONG

SAINT/LONG DEBATE POSTPONED INDEFINITELY

The much-anticipated debate between District 13 State House Representative candidates George Saint and Shen Long, scheduled to occur later this week, has been postponed, with no indication of when it might be rescheduled.

"I'm ready to move forward," Long responded when asked for comment. "My opponent's the one who's stalling. If you ask me, he's not prepared to talk about the issues and doesn't want to admit it."

George Saint requested the postponement days after a judge awarded Shen Long $1.7 million in damages in a lawsuit brought over the anti-cryptid language in Saint's ad campaign.

An official statement released by the Saint campaign calls the postponing of the debate "coincidental," explaining the candidate made an independent decision to embark on a pilgrimage "to pray for wisdom in the face of my opponent's underhanded attempts to discredit me."

This postponement is the capstone on what has been a difficult week for Saint. His courtroom loss, announced Monday, forced him to pull his most prominent ad campaign in addition to paying Long monetary damages. Two days later, a video that showed an irate Saint in the midst of an offensive anti-djinn rant at a local restaurant was posted to YouTube, receiving tens of thousands of views before it was removed.

As of last week, Long trailed Saint by almost ten points in the polls. Though popular with the city's young voters, Long—a 30-foot dragon, and the first of his species to receive a major party nomination—has yet to gain traction with voters in the 45-65 demographic. He polls surprisingly low with those aged 100 and above, as well, despite being the oldest candidate by far to ever run in a state election, at 358.

"My opponent is afraid to face me. That's what it comes down to," Long told reporters. "He knows this debate is my chance to show his supporters what I stand for, and he's worried they'll like what they hear. It's disturbing to see such fear of the truth from a self-described Knight of Virtue."

Representatives of the Saint campaign could not be reached for comment.

Creature Feature (On Channel 6 Morning News)

Channel 6: And it's time again for my favorite segment, where we welcome Edna from the Paws and Claws Rescue Center to showcase some of the adorable animals they have waiting for adoption. How are you doing today, Edna?

Edna: I'm just fantastic, Wendy. Absolutely thrilled to be back here with you this morning.

Channel 6: And you've brought some friends.

Edna: Yes, some very playful friends, as you can see. Sorry about that.

Channel 6: Oh, it's fine. These shoes were about to be out of season anyway. [laughs]

Edna: Well since this little lady is insisting on attention we'll start with her. Bastet here is just about the friendliest cat we've ever had at the Center. She acts more like a dog in a lot of ways—we've even taught her to play fetch!

Channel 6: She seems pretty calm around dogs, too.

Edna: She is—although that's not a dog. That's Chico, one of four Chupacabra puppies at the center currently.

Channel 6: You know that is reassuring to hear because when I looked at him, I couldn't help thinking he looked a little sick.

Edna: That's one of the reasons Chupacabras are so hard to find forever homes for. This kind of fur loss on a dog would be a sure sign of mange, but for a Chupacabra it's a perfectly normal pattern, and Chico and his litter-mates are all verified healthy and have their full shots.

Channel 6: Now for any views unfamiliar with the species, are Chupacabras expensive to feed?

Edna: Not at all. Feed them high-protein dog food and supplement it with blood, which you can get pretty cheap at any undead grocer. As far as care, Chupacabras need the same things you'd give to any canine—daily walks, an occasional bath, and lots of love.

Channel 6: Well he does seem like an affectionate little guy. Now we're running short on time so maybe we should meet your third friend—

Edna: Absolutely! I brought Baron, here, because I wanted to make a point that not all of our adoptable friends are mammalian! Baron is a 24-year-old Golden Griffin.

Channel 6: And what is the lifespan of a griffin? Because 24 would be pretty old for your average household pet.

Edna: Griffins have lifespans similar to people, so Baron's got a lot of happy years ahead of him. And he's incredibly well-trained, too. He was a seeing-eye bird before making his way to the Center.

Channel 6: You know, I've heard that griffin feathers restore sight to the blind.

Edna: Right you are, Wendy! He's also an ideal companion for single folks because he doesn't mind solitude and is very self-reliant. And while he's not completely hypoallergenic—he does still have some fur on his back—he's not as likely to trigger allergies as fuzzier pets.

Channel 6: And I see chess is listed here as one of his talents?

Edna: He gives me a run for my money most games. And I think he's unbeaten at Connect 4.

Channel 6: So a perfect match for any board game lovers out there, is what you're saying. We're just about out of time, Edna, so I want to remind the viewers the contact info for Paws and Claws is on the screen now and also on the Channel 6 website if you want to adopt any of the animals you've seen today.

Next up on Channel 6 morning news: the blurry security camera footage of an unidentifiable, loping figure that led to the arrest of a bigfoot subject has now been debunked as a hoax. We'll talk about what ramifications this might have for law enforcement when we come back.

6 Micro-Aggressions You Only Get If You're a Cryptid

Humans, right? Can't live with 'em, can't eat 'em. Kidding, of course—but even smart humans can say some ignorant shit. If you're a cryptid with humans in your life, I'll bet you've encountered at least one of these in the wild:

#1: "Can I touch your feathers/fur/scales?"
And, honestly, it's a step up when people even ask. No joke, I've had people come up and ruffle my feathers, and then ask if it's okay if they pet my dog (because apparently Chompers has more right to consent than I do).

#2: "How do you have sex/go to the bathroom/some other embarrassing thing I'd never ask a human?"

Most humans get to start small talk at their favorite food or what music they listen to. I spend my conversations with new people talking about whether I lay eggs and what color my poop is. Not exactly the basis of a quality connection.

#3: "You're a werewolf? Oh my god, I love the Thriller video!"

Insert pop culture reference here (bonus points for asking if you know fictional characters). While some cryptids aren't as bothered by this—comparing a vampire to Blade never fails to stroke their ego—for most it's one of the more annoying conversational points to respond to.

#4: "Do you guys really drink blood/eat souls/snatch children?"

The weirdest thing about this one is how disappointed a lot of people seem once they realize your life isn't built around murdering innocents.

#5: "But you're a harpy, how do you not like birds?"
Humans really like putting things in neat boxes, is all I can figure, and some of them can't seem to wrap their head around, for example, a vegetarian minotaur, tone-deaf siren, or selkie who can't swim. The best are the people who assume you're joking and proceed to get you a pet lorikeet because you'll obviously bond super hard.

#6: "My college roommate's boyfriend's brother dated a harpy for a couple months six years ago, do you know them?"
I appreciate the aspirational attitude here, imagining cryptids have this beautiful worldwide community that makes us all friends. The reality is, though, I'm as likely to have met your peripheral acquaintance who maybe lives in Omaha as you are to have met the Pope.

Comments on "6 Micro-Aggressions You Only Get if You're a Cryptid"

Darrell8989

My personal contribution: I'm a bigfoot working in a mostly-human office. A coworker keeps inviting me out to the movies (in a clear bid to get access to my Scarlet Dragons season tickets). Among his selections so far have been King Kong, Planet of the Apes, and a 25th-anniversary showing of Congo. *facepalm*

> **AmenhotepIX**
> You think that's bad? Try being a mummy who grew up in the '90s.
>
> **XOStormSwift**
> At least you get free movie tickets out of it.
>
> **ACharmingPrince**
> Why don't you just…not go?

LostLamb6525

Maybe if you all weren't so PISSY every time somebody asks a question you won't have to deal with all of these "microaggressions" (which is such a snowflake word I can't even). Like you're a half-bird-half-woman freak and I'm wrong for having questions? SMH.

L4dyL4z4ru$

Oh please. There's a very clear difference between "I'm curious about your unique culture" and all of the obviously offensive points OP outlined.

FieryFreja5

Don't feed the trolls.…

JustGort1111

Um…maybe a different word on a cryptid-friendly thread? Kthx from an actual troll who's completely on board with everything else in this post.

LostLamb6525

TROLL?!? I am a HUMAN and PROUD of it. I hope Saint slays ALL of you MONSTERS (yes, I said it!!!)

Matt869581112

I simply wanted to write down a quick word to say this is a very important matter you've brought to the attention of your readers. Thank you for the wonderful information you are sharing with your readers. I've got some news to share, as well! Something that has completely turned my life around and made me happier and more fulfilled in my bedroom and my confidence.

It's called CentaurX and it really works, guys, I'm serious. You're going to get a bigger size and more stamina in just hours after you start taking this natural supplement. Basically think about the phrase "hung like a…" and you know what centaurs are half of, right?

Here's the real secret though, guys, is that right now you can try it out for two months basically free if you just type in the code CRX60 when you checkout at CentaurX.com. Not sure how long it's going to last at those prices so hit it up now!

WINNER DECLARED IN 13th DISTRICT REPRESENTATIVE RACE

Incumbent George Saint has won the race for 13th District State House Representative, the local election board reported Wednesday morning.

According to election officials, Saint has secured 55% of the District 13 votes, compared to the 43% in favor of opponent Shen Long, with fewer than 5,000 ballots still to be counted. Long conceded shortly after results were released this morning, saying, "We may have lost this contest, but we should not view this as a failure. No cryptid candidate has received this level of support from any major party and I consider this just the first step in a longer quest."

Long, who is a 30-foot western dragon, called his visibility in the race a moral victory for cryptids everywhere. When asked if he would run for office in the future, Long said, "I plan on it, no question. I'm not even 400 yet. I feel like I'm just reaching my prime."

Long said this is not yet something he's focusing on, however, adding, "I've been working for our community without holding public office for decades, and that's always my first priority. As we saw from the brownie strike last spring, there is still plenty of work to be done on the ground to fight for rights for all of our citizens, and that's where I'll be focusing my energy in the months to come."

Saint also spoke following the election board's announcement, calling his win "a victory for moral fortitude." This will be Saint's fifth term as the 13th District Representative.

Overheard Conversation Between Two Bar Owners at the Riff Raff Club

"I mean, we all know the advantages," the first says. "Who else will work for baked goods? And you can't complain about their cleaning. Impeccable."

"Feels like there's a but coming," the second says.

The first answers, "It just feels like a hell of a risk."

They're side by side at the bar, watching a brownie bus a booth along the side wall. The brownie hums a jaunty tune as he makes a tower of the dirty glasses, stacking the plates with supernatural speed. The dishes are hardly on the tray before the table is wiped clean and sparkling.

The second man says, "I had one go bogart on me once."

"And you still use them?"

"Honestly, it wasn't too bad."

The first sends him a skeptical side-eye. "What'd it do?"

"The usual pranks. Sugar in the salt shakers, walk-in doors propped open, Jell-O congealed in the back of every toilet." The second man shrugs and says, "I mean, it wasn't pretty. Plumbers had to come snake the drains, threw out a freezer full of spoiled food. Even adding it all up, though, I still came out ahead compared to hiring human staff."

A second brownie comes out from the back carrying a tray of steaming clean glasses. Or maybe the same brownie; they're so hard to tell apart, and they move so damned fast.

"What set the little guy off?" the first man asks.

"One of the dishwashers ate his night's pay," the second answers. "New guy. Thought it was waste free for the taking. I started putting the brownie's pastries in a locked display case after that. Haven't had a problem since."

The first shakes his head, newly resolute. "That's what gets me, though. Any other staff member freaks out like that and they'd be out the door. Seems like a double-standard."

"To be fair, human staff would throw a fit, too, if somebody stole their paycheck."

The men contemplate their drinks. The brownie scurries off, back toward the kitchen, the glasses he'd brought out already neatly stacked behind the bar.

Jess Simms is a freelance writer from Pittsburgh, PA, where they're a cofounder of Scribble House and the managing editor of *After Happy Hour Review*. Their work can be found in Rinky Dink Press' series 10 of micro-chaps (*Shapeshifter Diaries*, 2023), as well as the 2022 *Nivalis Anthology* and *Bardic Tales and Sage Advice Vol. X*, among other publications. You can check out their blog and read more of their stories at JessSimms.com.

The title and page number font used in this book is Raven Scream, created by Sinister Fonts.

The page header font is Beat My Guest, created by Typodermic Fonts.